"**Jill Murphy deserves a constellation of gold stars for con**
picture books that please children and enrapture parents.'

When Jill Murphy penned the first of the Large
Family series over 30 years ago, little did she know
that her elephants would speak to so many, the
stories going on to sell over five million copies
worldwide. Today, numerous awards
and a television adaptation later, they
ring as true as ever, and continue to
be celebrated for their beautifully
observed depiction of hectic, warm —
but ultimately ordinary — family life.

THIS BOOK BELONGS TO:

....

First published 1987 by Walker Books Ltd
87 Vauxhall Walk, London SE11 5HJ

This edition published 2017

2 4 6 8 10 9 7 5 3 1

© 1987 Jill Murphy

The right of Jill Murphy to be identified as
author/illustrator of this work has been asserted by her
in accordance with the Copyright, Designs and Patents Act 1988

This book has been typeset in Bembo Educational

Printed in China

British Library Cataloguing in Publication Data:
a catalogue record for this book is available from the British Library

ISBN 978-1-4063-7074-4

www.walker.co.uk

All In One Piece

Jill Murphy

WALKER BOOKS
AND SUBSIDIARIES
LONDON • BOSTON • SYDNEY • AUCKLAND

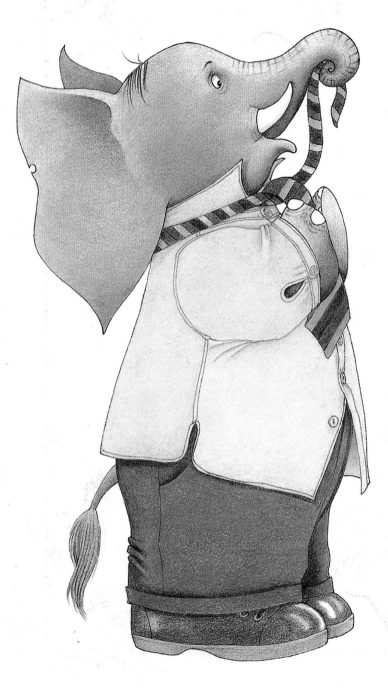

Mr Large was getting ready for work.
"Don't forget the office dinner-dance
tonight, dear," he said.
"Of course I won't," said Mrs Large.
"I've been thinking about it all year."

"Are children allowed at the dinner-dance?"
  asked Lester.

"No," said Mrs Large. "It'll be too late
  for little ones."

"What about the baby?" asked Luke.

"Granny is coming to take care of everyone,"
  said Mrs Large, "so there's no need to worry."

Granny arrived at tea time. The children
were already bathed and in their nightclothes.
Granny gave them some painting to do while
she tidied up and Mr and Mrs Large went
upstairs to get ready.

Luke sneaked into the bathroom while
Mr Large was shaving.
"Will I have to shave when I grow up?"
he asked, patting foam onto his trunk.
"Go away," said Mr Large. "I don't want
you ruining my best trousers!"

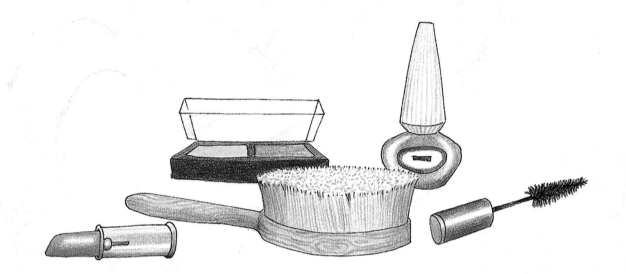

The baby crept into the bedroom where
Mrs Large was putting on her make-up.
Mrs Large didn't notice until it was too late.

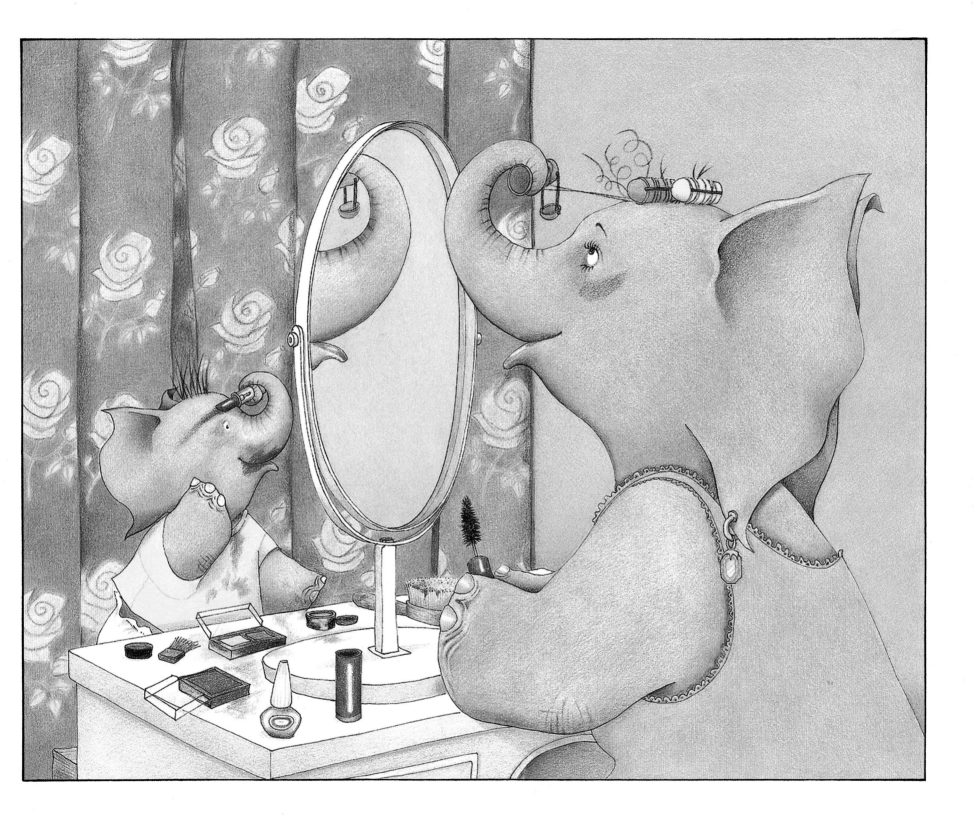

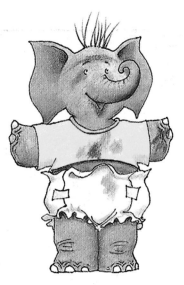

"Look!" said the baby. "Pretty!"

"Don't move," said Mrs Large. "Don't touch *anything*!"

Outside on the landing, things were even worse. Laura was clopping about in her mother's best shoes and beads and Lester and Luke were seeing how many toys they could cram into her new tights.

"Downstairs at *once*!" bellowed Mrs Large.
"Can't I have just one night in the whole year
   to myself? One night when I am not covered in
   jam and poster-paint? One night when I can put
   on my new dress and walk through the front
   door all in one piece?"

The children went downstairs to Granny.
Mr Large followed soon after, very smart
in his best suit. At last, Mrs Large
appeared in the doorway.
"How do I look?" she asked.

"Pretty, Mummy!" gasped the children.

"What a smasher!" said Mr Large.

"You look like a film star, dear,"
    said Granny.

"Hands off!" said Mrs Large to the
    paint-smeared children.

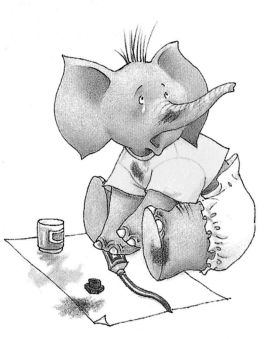

Mr and Mrs Large got ready to leave.

"Goodbye everyone," they said. "Be good now."

The baby began to cry.

"Just go," said Granny, picking her up.

"She'll stop as soon as you've left. Have a

lovely time."

"We've escaped," said Mr Large with a smile,
closing the front door behind them.

"All in one piece," said Mrs Large, "and
not a smear of paint between us."

"Actually," said Mr Large gallantly, "you'd
look wonderful to me, even if you were
covered in paint."

Which was perfectly true ...
and just as well really!

JILL MURPHY

is one of Britain's most treasured author-illustrators, who created her first book, the bestselling *The Worst Witch*, while still only eighteen. She is best known for her award-winning Large Family series – a series which includes *Five Minutes' Peace* and the Kate Greenaway shortlisted *A Quiet Night In.*

Among Jill's very popular characters are a small monster called Marlon, who appears in the acclaimed picture books *The Last Noo-Noo* and *All For One*, and Ruby the bunny, who stars in *Meltdown!* Jill lives in Cornwall.

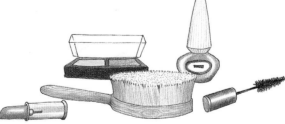